Major
TAYLOR

BY J. P. MILLER

ILLUSTRATED BY MARKIA JENAI

Rourke
Educational Media

A Division of
Carson
Dellosa
Education®

BEFORE AND DURING READING ACTIVITIES

Before Reading: *Building Background Knowledge and Vocabulary*

Building background knowledge can help children process new information and build upon what they already know. Before reading a book, it is important to tap into what children already know about the topic. This will help them develop their vocabulary and increase their reading comprehension.

Questions and Activities to Build Background Knowledge:

1. Look at the front cover of the book and read the title. What do you think this book will be about?
2. What do you already know about this topic?
3. Take a book walk and skim the pages. Look at the table of contents, photographs, captions, and bold words. Did these text features give you any information or predictions about what you will read in this book?

Vocabulary: *Vocabulary Is Key to Reading Comprehension*

Use the following directions to prompt a conversation about each word.

- Read the vocabulary words.
- What comes to mind when you see each word?
- What do you think each word means?

Vocabulary Words:
- advertise
- buggies
- cycling
- endurance
- Great Depression
- mentor
- monument
- professional

During Reading: *Reading for Meaning and Understanding*

To achieve deep comprehension of a book, children are encouraged to use close reading strategies. During reading, it is important to have children stop and make connections. These connections result in deeper analysis and understanding of a book.

 Close Reading a Text

During reading, have children stop and talk about the following:

- Any confusing parts
- Any unknown words
- Text to text, text to self, text to world connections
- The main idea in each chapter or heading

Encourage children to use context clues to determine the meaning of any unknown words. These strategies will help children learn to analyze the text more thoroughly as they read.

When you are finished reading this book, turn to the next-to-last page for **Text-Dependent Questions** and an **Extension Activity**.

TABLE OF CONTENTS

A RACE TO THE FINISH LINE

Have you ever tried to win a contest? Have you ever worked hard to reach a goal? Marshall "Major" Taylor understood how that felt. He knew what it meant to work hard and be determined.

Major zoomed around the track on his trusty bicycle. He knew he must be close to the finish line. He had been riding for a long time. He was in an **endurance** race that was supposed to last six days. He had not been in many races, but he was already a leader in this one. With hard work, he would become a leader in sports history too.

A STAR IN TRAINING

Major Taylor was born in 1878. He became best friends with the son of his father's boss. As a gift, the family gave Major a bicycle. Around and around in circles Major rode. He raced up ramps and down stairs. Major loved his new bicycle. He had not owned it long, but he was already good at doing tricks with it.

Bicycles had not been around for very long at the time. More people were starting to use them instead of horses and **buggies**. The owner of the Hay and Willits bicycle shop hired Major to **advertise** bikes and teach people to ride them. At the shop, Major did bicycle tricks in an attention-getting soldier's uniform. People gave him the nickname "Major" because of his uniform.

Making Money

Major made $6 a week at his job at the bicycle shop. He also got a free bike worth $35.

The owner of the bicycle shop got a big idea. He would enter Major in a race 10 miles (about 16 kilometers) long to advertise the shop. However, he only wanted Major to finish the first mile.

Major went to the race not knowing what to expect. There was a pack of riders at the starting line. He was the only African American rider.

The race started. Major pumped his pedals as fast as he could. As he rode, he **passed riders going uphill, ...passed them at the one-mile mark, ...and passed them to cross the finish line.**

At age 13, Major had won his first bicycle race. It was only the beginning.

Major knew he could be a winner. He wanted to learn how. A **cycling** club in his hometown would only allow white members. He and other African American riders formed the See-Saw Cycling Club instead.

His racing victory got the attention of Louis "Birdie" Munger. He owned a bicycle company. He became Major's **mentor**. Birdie wanted Major to do a short **professional** race. If he won, he could enter another race that would last six days. Major was only 18 years old. He had never entered a professional race before. If he could do this, many more great things could be in his future.

Major sped to victory in the first race. Next up was the big, six-day endurance race at Madison Square Garden, an indoor arena in New York City. The race started with 28 cyclists. Some white people did not like that a black man was racing along with them. But Major did not let that stop him.

The race was very difficult. By the second day, Major could no longer keep the same speed. He began racing for eight hours and resting for one hour. His stomach hurt. His head hurt. On the fifth day, a white cyclist who did not like that a black man was racing made him crash. Still, he kept pedaling his bike.

Over those six days, Major rode 1,732 miles (about 2,787 kilometers). He finished in eighth place. This was incredible for someone who had not done this kind of race before.

MAKING HISTORY

That race was only the beginning. Soon, Major had set seven world records. He became the first African American to win a world championship in cycling. He became famous. He did not stop even when white riders did things like throw ice water in his face during a race. He gave other black cyclists hope that they could succeed too.

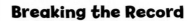

Breaking the Record

In 1899, Major biked a mile in 1 minute and 19 seconds. He set a new world record. People called him "The Fastest Man in the World."

For 14 years, Major Taylor continued to be a leader in cycling. He retired from the sport at age 32 and moved to Chicago, Illinois. Major had earned a lot of money from cycling. Unfortunately, he lost almost all of it because of the **Great Depression**. When he died in 1932, he had no money, and not many people knew about him. He did not even have a gravestone at the cemetery where he was buried. This important leader seemed to have been lost to history.

But Major Taylor would not be forgotten after all. People honored him as a leader after he died. In 1948, a group of cyclists told a bicycle company owner about Major's life. The owner paid for Major's grave to be moved and marked. Several cycling clubs host events to honor his life each year. There is even a **monument** to him in Worcester, Massachusetts. He was more than a leader in races. He was a leader in sports and history as well.

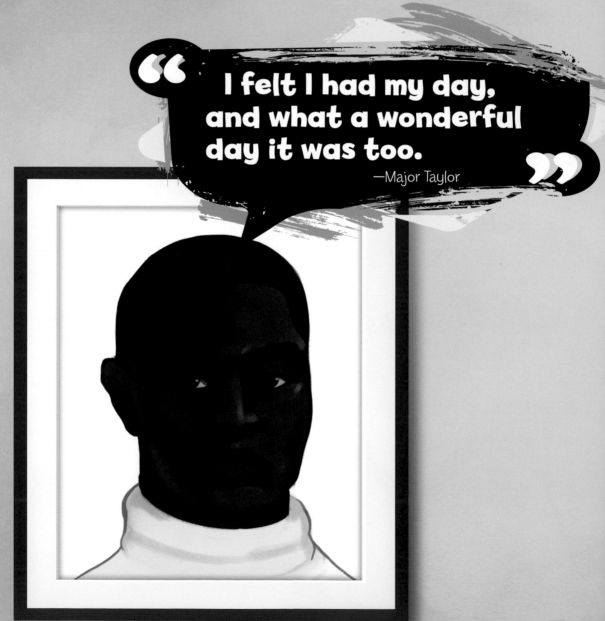

" I felt I had my day, and what a wonderful day it was too.
—Major Taylor "

TIME LINE

1878 Marshall "Major" Taylor is born to Saphronia Kelter Taylor and Gilbert Taylor in Indianapolis, Indiana.

1886–1890 Major lives with the Southard family and is tutored with their son. He is given his first bicycle in 1890 by the Southard family.

1891 Major is hired by Tom Hay to perform bicycle tricks in front of the Hay and Willits bicycle shop for $6 a week.

1892 13-year-old Major is entered in a bicycle race to advertise for the Hay and Willits bicycle shop.

1895 Louis D. "Birdie" Munger, owner of Munger Cycle Manufacturing, meets Major. Major moves to Worcester, Massachusetts.

1896 Major participates in a six-day endurance race in Madison Square Garden and places eighth.

1898 Major holds seven world records at this point.

1899 Major wins the Montreal World Championship Professional 1-mile (1.6-kilometer) race at Queens Park.

1902 Major enters 57 races of the European Tour and wins 40 of them, defeating the champions of Germany, England, and France.

1903 A huge bicycle race is created in Australia to attract Major Taylor to compete.

1910 Major retires from track racing.

1932 Major dies in the charity ward of Cook County Hospital Chicago on June 21st. He is buried in an unmarked grave.

1948 A group of former professional bike racers work together to honor Major by giving him a proper burial.

GLOSSARY

advertise (AD-vur-tize): to give information about something that you want to promote or sell

buggies (BUHG-eez): lightweight carriages with two wheels pulled by a horse

cycling (SYE-kling): related to riding a bicycle

endurance (en-DOOR-uhns): the ability to do something difficult for a long time

Great Depression (grayt di-PRESH-uhn): a time in the 1930s when many people did not have jobs and had little food or money

mentor (MEN-tor): a person who teaches and guides another person

monument (MAHN-yuh-muhnt): a statue, building, or other structure that reminds people of an event or person

professional (pruh-FESH-uh-nuhl): making money for doing something others do for fun

INDEX

TEXT-DEPENDENT QUESTIONS

1. Why did Marshall Taylor get the nickname "Major"?

2. What did Major Taylor do at the bicycle shop?

3. What was the name of the bicycle club Major Taylor joined?

4. What happened to Major Taylor after he retired?

5. How was Major Taylor honored in Worcester, Massachusetts?

EXTENSION ACTIVITY

Set up a mini bike rodeo to teach friends how to ride bicycles safely. Research bicycle safety tips. Set up an obstacle course for riders to test their skills. What supplies will you need? Whose help do you need? Make sure your bike rodeo is fun and educational.

ABOUT THE AUTHOR

J. P. Miller is a debut author in children's picture books. She is eager to write stories about little- and well-known African American leaders. She hopes that her stories will augment the classroom experience, educate, and inspire readers. J. P. lives in Metro Atlanta, Georgia, and enjoys playing pickleball and swimming in her spare time.

ABOUT THE ILLUSTRATOR

Markia Jenai was raised in Detroit during rough times, but she found adventure through art and storytelling. She grew up listening to old stories of her family members, which gave her an interest in history. Drawing was her way of exploring the world through imagination.

www.rourkeeducationalmedia.com

Quote source: Taylor, Major. *The Fastest Bicycle Rider in the World: The Autobiography of Major Taylor.* Brattleboro, VT: S. Greene Press, 1972.

Edited by: Tracie Santos
Illustrations by: Markia Jenai
Cover and interior layout by: Rhea Magaro-Wallace

Library of Congress PCN Data

Major Taylor / J. P. Miller
(Leaders Like Us)
ISBN 978-1-73163-802-1 (hard cover)
ISBN 978-1-73163-879-3 (soft cover)
ISBN 978-1-73163-956-1 (e-Book)
ISBN 978-1-73164-033-8 (ePub)
Library of Congress Control Number: 2020930059

Rourke Educational Media
Printed in the United States of America
01-1942011937